Snorlax Takes a Stand

Pokémon junior

#9

There are more books
about Pokémon for
younger readers.

COLLECT THEM ALL!

COMING SOON!

Snorlax Takes a Stand

POKéMON junior

#9

Adapted by S. E. Heller

SCHOLASTIC INC.
New York   Toronto   London   Auckland   Sydney
Mexico City   New Delhi   Hong Kong

ISBN 0-439-20098-9

12 11 10 9 8   7 8 9/9 0 1 2/0

Printed in the U.S.A.

First Scholastic printing, March 2001

CHAPTER ONE

Looking for Food

Splash! Pikachu got wet. The little yellow Pokémon and its human friends could not leave the island today. The sea was too stormy.

"We will have to find food," said Misty. Misty was a good friend of Ash, Pikachu's trainer. She went

with Ash and Pikachu on all their travels.

Tracey pointed to some flowers. "These should be okay for the Pokémon to eat," he said. Tracey was another friend of Ash's. He liked to watch Pokémon and draw them.

Tracey pulled and tugged at the flowers.

"Ouch!" said a voice. Out of the grass came a boy. The flowers were growing out of his head.

"I am sorry," said Tracey. "I thought I was picking weeds."

"Weeds?" yelled the boy. "How dare you! I am Gullzar, a Grass Pokémon trainer. This is my special garden."

Gullzar was so mad that he wanted to have a battle.

Ash tried to stop the fight. "We

are too hungry to have a battle," Ash told the angry Pokémon trainer.

Gullzar thought that Ash was afraid to battle. This was not true. Ash wanted to be a great Pokémon Master. Pikachu knew that he would never run from a battle. The match was on!

CHAPTER TWO

Poké Ball Problems

Gullzar took out a Poké Ball. He called Gloom, a Weed Pokémon that smelled really bad.

Ash called Charizard, a Fire Pokémon. Pikachu was surprised to see Squirtle instead. Squirtle looked like a turtle. It was a Water Pokémon. It wanted to join the

battle.

"Well, all right," said Ash. "Squirtle, use Water Gun!"

Squirtle sprayed Gloom with water. The Weed Pokémon jumped up and down with joy.

"Ash! What are you doing?" Misty cried. "Weed Pokémon love water. It helps them grow."

"I guess I am too hungry to think clearly," said Ash. "Return, Squirtle."

Now Ash took out another

Poké Ball. He swung his arm back to call Charizard. But the Poké Ball slipped. It fell from Ash's hand onto a rock.

"Snorlax?" cried the friends. The giant Sleeping Pokémon had come out of the Poké Ball. It was snoring loudly.

"Return, Snorlax," said Ash. Ash held the Poké Ball above the

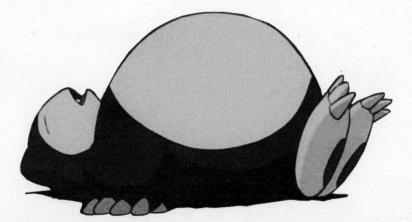

sleeping giant. But Snorlax did not return. The Poké Ball was broken!

Oh, no, thought Pikachu. Now Snorlax would have to battle Gloom. Could Ash get it to wake up?

CHAPTER THREE

The Hungry Giant

"Gloom, use Solar Beam!" cried Gullzar.

A light began to glow from the top of Gloom's head. It blasted Snorlax. The giant Pokémon was thrown backward.

"Ahh," yawned Snorlax. It opened its eyes and sniffed the air.

What was that smell? It was stinky, but Snorlax did not care. The giant Pokémon crawled toward the smell. *It must be something to eat,* thought Snorlax. With a giant chomp, Snorlax tried to eat the Weed Pokémon.

Gullzar screamed. He did not

want Gloom to be eaten. "Return, Gloom," he cried.

Still, Snorlax wanted food. It sniffed the air again. Then the giant Pokémon ate Gullzar's special garden — right off the boy's head!

Yum, thought Snorlax. It did not hear Gullzar yelling and crying. Snorlax was too busy smelling something else. There was more food. The smell was coming from the bag on Gullzar's back. Quickly, Snorlax grabbed Gullzar's lunch and ate it all up.

"Wah! Wah!" sobbed Gullzar. "This battle is over!"

Snorlax thought so, too. Its tummy was full. With a happy sigh, the Pokémon went back to sleep.

CHAPTER FOUR

The Thousand-Pound Problem

Ash needed to find a Pokémon Center. Snorlax's Poké Ball had to be fixed.

"Hah!" cried Gullzar. "The closest Pokémon Center is over those mountains."

"*Pika!*" cried Pikachu. How would the friends move Snorlax

over the mountains? The giant
Pokémon weighed more than a
thousand pounds.

"Serves you right!" laughed
Gullzar. He ran off.

The friends watched the boy
dance over the hills. What would
they do now?

First they tried rolling the
Sleeping Pokémon on logs. Ash,
Pikachu, and Tracey pulled a rope
attached to Snorlax. Misty ran
back and forth, sliding logs under
the big Pokémon.

This was hard work. The heavy

giant was not easy to roll. Soon they needed a break.

"*Pika pi,*" sighed Pikachu. It was tired and hungry.

"Look!" cried Tracey. An apple had fallen out of his backpack. Tracy had forgotten all about it!

Pikachu ran for a bite of the apple. So did Ash and Misty. They were so hungry, they could not wait to share the fruit.

"Wait," said Tracey. He had an idea. "We can use this apple to get Snorlax moving."

CHAPTER FIVE

An Apple of an Idea

Tracey put the apple on a string. He held the fruit near Snorlax's nose. His plan was to run with the apple, so Snorlax would wake up and follow him.

Sniff, sniff. Snorlax smelled the food. It opened its mouth. *Chomp!* Before Tracey could start running,

the apple was gone.

Now what would they do? Snorlax was asleep again and they had no more food.

"We can trick Snorlax," said Misty. "We can use a fake apple. If Snorlax thinks that it is real food, he will try to get it."

Pikachu laughed as Misty dressed up Ash to look like an apple. Snorlax would be sure to run after this giant treat!

Boom! Boom! The ground shook as Snorlax chased Ash up the mountain path. Pikachu could not believe how fast the huge Pokémon could run.

"Help!" cried Ash. Snorlax was running very, very fast! Ash turned to look at the Pokémon. But — oh, no — he tripped on a rock.

Snorlax grabbed the fake apple. It tried to bite the fruit. Yuck! Snorlax gave a cry and spit Ash out. Then the heavy Pokémon fell to the ground. Snorlax was asleep again.

CHAPTER SIX

Down the River

Pikachu ran to Ash. It was worried. Was Ash hurt?

"I am okay, Pikachu," said the boy. He sat up and smiled at his beloved Pokémon. Ash and Pikachu always looked out for each other.

"Thank goodness I taste bad,"

Ash said. Then he laughed.

Misty and Tracey joined the friends. Now they were on top of the mountain.

"Look," Misty pointed. She saw a river. "We can make a raft and float down to the Pokémon Center."

"Good idea," said Tracey.

Everyone pitched in to make the raft. Then they climbed on board.

"*Brrr*," said Togepi. Misty's little Pokémon was excited about the ride. It was fun to sail down the river!

Suddenly, the water started to

move faster. The raft was turning and bouncing!

"Oh, no!" cried Misty. "We are headed for a waterfall!"

"*Pika!*" cried Pikachu. *Oh, no!* The raft flew over the falls. It was a long way down. How would the friends survive?

"Aaaaah!" Tracey and Ash yelled. They were falling very, very fast.

But, luckily, Snorlax broke the fall. The large Pokémon landed

21

on his back. It did not even wake up when Ash, Tracey, Misty, and Pikachu bounced onto its stomach!

CHAPTER SEVEN

A Big Surprise

"Are you having fun?" laughed Gullzar. He was watching from the riverbank. Just a few yards away was the Pokémon Center.

"Hooray!" shouted the friends. They splashed to shore and happily rolled Snorlax onto some logs. They pulled it toward the center.

But when they got there, they saw a long line.

"Why are all of these people here?" asked Misty.

"Everyone is waiting for Pokémon food," said Gullzar. He was waiting for food, too. "A plane is bringing food and supplies from a nearby island. It will be here soon."

"*Pika!*" Pikachu pointed.

The plane flew over the Pokémon Center and dropped a box. Everyone watched as it floated down.

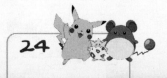

Then, suddenly, the crowd gasped. A rocket with a clamp on it hit the box and pulled it in another direction. Someone was stealing the food!

Pikachu ran with Ash. They had to find the thieves! Soon they had tracked them down. It was Team Rocket.

"I should have known!" cried Ash.

Whenever there was trouble, Team Rocket was behind it. They were always trying to steal Pokémon for their boss. Pikachu wondered what Jessie, James, and Meowth were up to now.

CHAPTER EIGHT

Metal Meowth

"Give back the food!" cried Ash.

Jessie smiled wickedly. "We will give you your food when you give us Pikachu," she said. Team Rocket knew Pikachu was special. They wanted it more than any other Pokémon.

"*Pikaaaa!*" cried the little yellow

Pokémon. *No way!*

Ash held Pikachu tight. "Do not worry, Pikachu," said Ash. "I will never hand you over."

Pikachu looked at the crowd. The Pokémon trainers were coming closer. They needed the food

for their Pokémon. Would they try to take Pikachu away from Ash?

"Step back!" Gullzar shouted at the islanders. "I know you are worried about your own Pokémon. Still, that is no excuse to put someone else's Pokémon in danger."

"*Pika*," said Pikachu. The little Pokémon was glad to have Gullzar on its side.

Now the crowd faced Team Rocket together.

Jessie and James stepped aside. Out came Meowth, their talking

Pokémon. It was wearing a metal suit. It had sharp blades instead of cat claws. It had a strong helmet and a body made of steel. Inside, Meowth pushed buttons to move the metal machine. *Clang, clang, clang* went the heavy feet.

"If you will not give us Pikachu, then Meowth will take it in a Pokémon battle," said James.

30

CHAPTER NINE

An Unfair Fight

Pikachu was mad at the bullies. It was unfair for Meowth to use special armor. But the little yellow Pokémon knew it had to fight Meowth.

"Use Thunderbolt!" cried Ash.

Pikachu jumped into the air. "*PIK-A-CHUUU!*" it cried. Its

Electric Attack hit Meowth's helmet. But the electricity went down
the metal suit and into the ground.
It was not working!

"You cannot hurt me, Pikachu,"
said Meowth. It started to chase
the Electric Pokémon. Meowth
was using Power Swipes.

"*Pika!*" cried Pikachu. Meowth's

sharp metal claws whipped around like fan blades. Pikachu barely jumped out of the way in time. The little yellow Pokémon was in trouble.

"Return, Pikachu!" cried Ash. "This is not a fair fight."

"If you give up, Meowth wins," said Jessie.

"And we get to take Pikachu," said James.

Pikachu looked at Team Rocket with anger. No one could beat that metal fighting machine! What could Ash and Pikachu do?

CHAPTER TEN

Snorlax Joins the Battle

Just then the ground began to shake. *Boom! Boom! Boom!* Snorlax was walking toward Meowth. Its eyes glowed red. Snorlax was ready for battle.

Meowth charged the giant Pokémon.

"Fury Swipes!" called Meowth.

34

The metal claws whipped around faster than ever.

Snorlax stood its ground until the last minute. Every time Meowth jumped forward, Snorlax jumped to the side.

"Hey! My hand is stuck!" cried Meowth. It was trying to hit Snorlax. But its metal claws had hit a rock instead.

Now Meowth tried a different attack. The metal helmet flew at Snorlax with rocket power.

Pop! The helmet bounced off Snorlax like a rubber ball. Snorlax

touched its head. Meowth could not believe it! Its attack had failed.

"Use Body Slam!" James told Meowth.

The talking Pokémon did not know which button to press in its suit. It hit the wrong one. Oops! Now the front of the suit fell off. Meowth shot out of the machine — right into Snorlax's belly.

Snorlax breathed in. Meowth was sucked into Snorlax's belly. It was trapped.

Then, with a deep breath, Snorlax popped Meowth out. The talking Pokémon shot toward Jessie and James. *Splash!* Meowth knocked Team Rocket right into the river!

CHAPTER ELEVEN

Hidden Talents

"All right, Snorlax!" cheered Ash. He was proud of his Pokémon.

"Snorlax has hidden talents," said Tracey.

The giant Pokémon was going to use a new attack. Its mouth started to glow.

"Wow!" said Ash. He did not

know that Snorlax knew how to use its Hyper Beam Attack.

With a forceful roar, Snorlax sent Team Rocket flying right off the island.

"Hooray!" cried the islanders.

Ash held out his arms to hug Snorlax. His eyes were tearing up.

"Great job, Snorlax," said Ash. "I am so touched that you would battle for me."

Boom! Boom! Boom! Snorlax ran toward Ash. And then it ran past him! It headed for the box of Pokémon food. It ripped off the

top. Snorlax ate until his stomach was full. Then, tired and happy, Snorlax fell back to sleep.

"*Pika pi,*" said Pikachu. *Oh, dear.* Snorlax had not battled for Ash. Snorlax had battled for food.

Ash shook his head. At least he had gotten the Poké Ball fixed.

"Return, Snorlax," said Ash. The sleeping hero flashed into the Poké Ball.

Pikachu was glad that it would not have to pull the giant Pokémon around anymore. And it was excited to begin a new adventure.

Gullzar met the friends before they left. "I was wrong," Gullzar told Ash. "You are a great Pokémon trainer. I would love to battle you again someday, especially against that Snorlax."

Pikachu smiled. It was glad that Ash and Gullzar were shaking hands. The Grass Pokémon trainer had turned out to be a real friend after all. Who would have guessed that Snorlax could start a friendship?

Will Lapras ever find its way home?

Pokémon junior

Chapter Book #10:
Good-bye, Lapras

Ash's Pokémon Lapras may be huge, but it's just a baby. Ash rescued it when it got lost from its herd. Now they want to return Lapras to its family. First they have to save the herd from attacking pirates. And to do that, they might need help from an unlikely source — Team Rocket!

Coming soon to a bookstore near you!
Visit us at www.scholastic.com